Magic Pony Carousel

Book 3

STAR
THE WESTERN PONY

Magic Pony Carousel

Book 3

STAR
THE WESTERN PONY

Poppy Shire

Illustrations by Ron Berg

HarperTrophy®

An Imprint of HarperCollins*Publishers*

★ ★ ★ ★ ★

STAR THE WESTERN PONY

Text copyright © 2007 by Working Partners

Illustrations copyright © 2007 by Ron Berg
www.harpercollinschildrens.com

Library of Congress Cataloging-in-Publication Data
Shire, Poppy.
    Star the western pony / by Poppy Shire ; illustrations by Ron
Berg. —1st Harper Trophy ed.
        p.   cm. — (The magic pony carousel ; bk. 3)
    Summary: Laura goes for a ride on a magic carousel that takes
her to the old West, where she and her pony and a new friend
save a herd of cattle from would-be rustlers.
    ISBN 978-0-06-083785-3
    [1. Cattle drives—Fiction. 2. Ponies—Fiction. 3. Space and
time—Fiction. 4. Magic—Fiction. 5. West (U.S.)—History—
Fiction.] I. Berg, Ron, ill. II. Title.
PZ7.S55795Sta 2007   2006103282
[Fic]—dc22   CIP
                                                      AC

Typography by Sasha Illingworth
◆
First Harper Trophy edition, 2007
★ ★ ★ ★ ★

With special thanks to Gill Harvey

Chapter 1

"**L**ook! It's a lasso game!" cried Laura. "Let's try that next!" She ran across the fairground, with her three brothers chasing her. They all loved anything to do with the Wild West! But Laura was the only one who also loved detective stories—she was always looking for a new mystery to solve.

As they waited in line to throw lassos over different prizes, Laura hopped from foot to foot. "Come *on*, come *on*," she chanted.

Suddenly she heard a voice booming across the fairground. "Step up, step up for the most exciting ride of your lives! Choose your favorite pony and let Barker's Magic Pony Carousel whisk you away on an amazing adventure! Ride a circus pony, a princess's pony, or a cowgirl's pony straight from the Wild West. . . ."

"Did you hear that?" Laura gasped. She loved riding ponies as much as she loved the Wild West. A cowgirl's pony sounded like the most exciting thing in the whole world! She looked hopefully at her oldest brother, Sam. "Can I ride the Magic Carousel, please?"

"You and your ponies." Sam grinned. "Okay. But I don't think the carousel's a ride for me. I'll just watch."

"Thanks!" said Laura.

They left Laura's middle brothers, Harry and Paul, in line for the lasso stall and made their way to Mr. Barker's Magic Carousel.

Close up, the carousel's twinkling lights

glowed merrily in the dusk of early evening. Laura stared at the swirling red, gold, and silver colors, desperate for a glimpse of the cowgirl's pony. There was the circus pony with a sparkly feather headdress and an Arabian horse that had a fiery glint in his eye. She saw the princess's pony with its neck proudly arched . . . but where was the cowgirl's pony?

Then Laura saw her. She was the most beautiful pony on the carousel! She was a rich golden chestnut color all over, apart from a star on her forehead and three pretty white socks. She wore a fancy leather bridle and a heavy tan Western saddle. She looked just like the ponies in Laura's favorite Western movies!

"Step up, step up!" called a tall man in a red-and-green striped top hat. "Choose your favorite pony!" He caught sight of Laura. "Hello, young lady! I'm Mr. Barker. Welcome to my magnificent Magic Carousel!"

Laura smiled. Mr. Barker had such friendly, twinkling eyes! "I think I know which pony I want," she said.

"Well, that's a good start. But has that pony been chosen for you?" asked Mr. Barker mysteriously.

Laura was puzzled. "I don't know," she said.

Mr. Barker laughed and lifted his striped top hat. There was a flash of pink paper as he pulled something out from under it. It was a ticket! Laura glanced at Sam to see if he'd seen how the ticket had appeared, but he was busy looking at the ponies on the carousel.

"This is yours," said Mr. Barker, handing her the ticket.

Laura looked at it. There was a name on it in swirling gold writing. "Star!" she read out breathlessly. The cowgirl's pony had a star on

her forehead—could that be her name? Feeling excited, she ran over to the carousel to take a closer look. The horse's name was written on her browband.

"It says Star here, too!" she said.

"Then that's the pony for you," said Mr. Barker.

Star's painted brown eyes seemed to be encouraging her, so Laura clambered quickly onto the carousel. The Western saddle was very different from the English saddles she was used to. It was much more complicated, with a big horn at the front, lots of ropes and leather pouches, and stirrups that were much lower. But as the carousel began to turn, Laura felt so safe and comfortable that it was as if she'd always known how to ride a cowgirl's pony.

Laura waved at Sam, who grinned and waved back. The carousel music grew louder, and the horses swooped through the air as they gathered speed. The breeze blew on Laura's cheeks, and the fairground lights seemed to glitter and twinkle around her. To her surprise the breeze felt warm, like on a summer's day, and the air began to glow and shimmer like a summery mist. She looked up and gasped. It was no longer a cool autumn evening. Instead, the sky was a beautiful bright blue, with the sun blazing down. And she wasn't holding on to the golden pole anymore. She had real leather reins in one hand and a rope lasso in the other!

Laura blinked. When she opened her eyes again, she could see Star's chestnut mane flying in the breeze. Dust swirled around her, and the sound of thundering hooves filled her ears. Her jacket had disappeared. Instead, she was wearing a pink-and-white-checked shirt with the sleeves rolled up, denim jeans, and beautiful pale leather cowboy boots. The fairground had gone, and she was cantering beside a long line of cattle that stretched far ahead across a rolling plain. The cattle were all colors—brown and white, speckled and patchy—and they all had big, dangerous-looking horns.

Laura shielded her eyes against the sun. She could see a river up ahead, and in the distance rocky mountains jutted into the sky. There were other riders cantering beside the cattle, too, wearing wide-brimmed hats and long leather chaps.

"Wow!" Laura exclaimed. "It's a Wild West cattle drive!"

Chapter 2

Laura didn't have time to wonder how she'd gotten here. Some of the cattle were bellowing loudly, and she wanted to keep a close eye on those pointy horns! She concentrated on holding her reins. It was tricky having them in just one hand, but she remembered from watching Western movies that she had to rest the reins against the pony's neck to tell her which way to go.

Just as she was getting the hang of it, she heard a shout from behind her. Alarmed, she looked around. There was a girl galloping toward

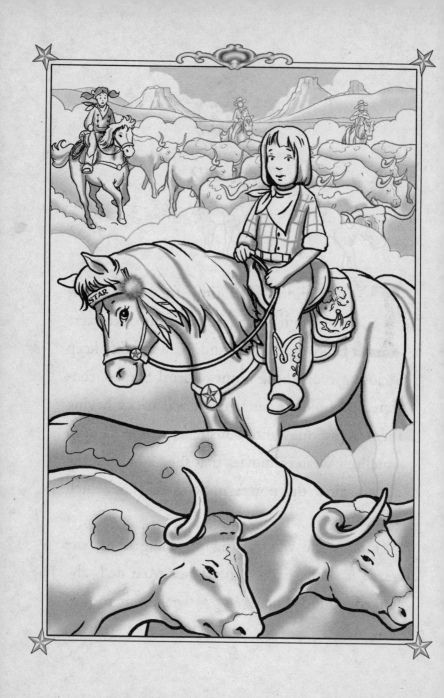

her on a brown-and-white pony, and she looked very cross! She was wearing a buttercup-yellow shirt, and her glossy black pigtails were tied with yellow ribbons.

Laura opened her mouth to speak, but she didn't get a chance.

"Rope that calf!" cried the girl, pointing past Laura. "What are you waiting for?"

Laura twisted around and saw a young calf bolting away from the rest of the herd. Its spindly legs were a blur as it raced off in a panic—straight toward the river!

Gripping her lasso tighter, Laura wheeled Star after the calf and kicked her into a gallop. She looked down at the rope in her right hand. It was much heavier than the lasso rope she played with at home. "I'm not sure I'm going to be able to catch the calf," she muttered to herself.

"Swing . . . it around . . . a few times . . ." said

a breathless voice, "before you throw it!"

Laura glanced around, but there was no one there. Just herself and Star, galloping after the calf.

"It's me . . . Star!" puffed the voice, as the pony's hooves thundered across the dry, hard ground. "We've come here by magic . . . from the carousel. We have something very important to do . . . before I take you back!"

Laura nearly fell out of the saddle in surprise. "Star!" she gasped. "You can talk!"

"Hurry up!" shouted the girl with pigtails. Laura looked over her shoulder and saw that the brown-and-white pony was catching up.

The calf was getting closer and closer to the river. Laura knew she didn't have time to ask Star any questions about the carousel. Somehow, she had to get the hang of using her lasso. She leaned sideways out of the saddle and stretched her hand toward the calf. The rope felt even heavier now!

"Quick, or you'll lose him!" called the girl.

"Ignore her," panted Star. "Just concentrate on the rope. . . . It's all about . . . timing. I'll try not to . . . frighten the calf."

Laura's heart was pounding wildly. The calf looked so small and helpless, and she could hear him calling out in fear. He was only a few paces from the river now, which looked big and wide with swirling currents of fast-flowing, muddy water. Laura noticed a branch being swept along, until it smashed against a boulder. The calf wouldn't stand a chance if he fell in!

"Please stop, little calf," Laura pleaded. "Please!"

But the calf kept on running. Then, just as he was about to plunge into the river, he skidded to a halt on the muddy bank.

Star stopped at once. "I don't want to startle him," she whispered to Laura. "You should be able to rope him from here."

Laura glanced behind her. The brown-and-white pony had stopped, too, but he was stamping restlessly, tugging at the bit.

"I can't come any closer!" called the girl. "If I do, I'll frighten the calf even more. You'll have to rope him yourself!"

Laura nodded. The calf stood with his tiny hooves sinking into the mud at the edge of the river. His big brown eyes were wide with fear.

"Stay there," Laura murmured, lifting the lasso. "Just stay right there!"

She lifted the lasso and began to swing it around above her head, feeling the coil of rope spin faster and faster through the air. But just as she was about to throw it, the other girl's pony kicked a stone and sent it clattering toward the river. With

a bleat of panic, the calf plunged straight into the swirling water!

Laura kicked Star forward at once. The calf was already being swept downstream, his head only just above the surface. With a brave whinny, Star splashed into the river and Laura flung the lasso as hard as she could.

"I've got him!" she cried, as the rope slipped over the calf's neck and shoulders.

"Now wind the rope around the saddle horn," instructed Star. "I'll try to dig my hooves into the mud while you pull him in."

Beneath her, Laura could feel the pony struggling to keep her balance. The current was almost too strong for a sturdy cowgirl's pony, never mind a calf! Laura heaved on the rope, winding it around the strong piece of leather at the front of Star's saddle. The wet rope dug into her fingers, but she kept on pulling.

Suddenly Star slipped, and Laura lurched forward.

"Oh no!" she gasped, as the rope dragged through her fingers and the calf bobbed farther away.

"It's okay," muttered Star, through gritted teeth. "I've got my footing now. Don't give up!"

Laura hauled on the rope again. It felt as though her arms were going to drop off, and the calf didn't seem any nearer! She could hear shouts from behind her, but they were muffled by the roar of the river. Inch by inch, Star slowly stepped back toward the bank. At last she was wading out of the water onto dry land. Laura gave a few final tugs on the rope and the calf stumbled out of the river on trembling legs.

Laura swung herself out of the saddle and flung her arms around Star's neck. The mare was still out of breath and her nostrils were flaring, but her eyes were friendly and calm.

"Thank you so much!" Laura whispered. Then she turned to the calf and hugged him, too. The calf gave a grateful lick to the back of Laura's hand. His coat was soaked and muddy but she didn't care. He was safe, thanks to Laura and Star, and that was all that mattered!

Chapter 3

"**W**ell done!" cried a voice, and Laura looked up. A cowboy was walking toward her wearing a big gray hat and dusty, well-worn jeans. He was leading his horse, which was a strong-looking bay with a stripe down his face. "We saw what happened," he said. "You were really brave to go into the river!"

Laura hugged the small calf one last time. He had stopped shivering, and his big brown eyes no longer looked afraid. She stood up and placed her hand on Star's warm chestnut neck. Six or seven other men followed the cowboy in the gray hat. They looked like characters from the Western movies that Laura watched with her brothers, with their tanned faces, brown leather cowboy boots, and long chaps.

"You've made a great start," Star whispered in Laura's ear.

Laura grinned. But Star's words reminded her that no one knew who she was. How was she going to explain where she'd come from?

"We'll take this little fella to join the others," said the first cowboy. "Then we'll all rest up over there before we move off." He nodded down-river, and Laura saw a huddle of wooden build-ings not far away.

He held Star's reins while Laura climbed back into the saddle. "My name's Luke," he said. "I don't think we've met before."

"Er . . . no," stammered Laura. "I— I live over

there." She pointed toward the wooden houses, and heard Star snort in approval.

"Well, I'm the head cowboy," said Luke. "You've already met my daughter Jolene." He nodded toward the girl in the yellow shirt.

"My name's Laura," she said. She smiled at Jolene, but to her surprise, Jolene just scowled and turned her pony away.

With the calf trotting beside them, Laura and Star followed the other cowboys back to the slow-moving line of cattle. The calf was already looking much happier! An older cowboy rode up on a pretty dun-colored mustang.

"Well done," he said warmly. "You did really well to save that calf."

Laura jumped. He sounded just like Mr. Barker from the fairground! She stared up at him curiously. He had wisps of white hair showing underneath his wide-brimmed felt hat and twinkling blue eyes. He *looked* just like Mr. Barker, too!

She was about to ask him what his name was when the cowboy touched the brim of his hat in farewell and rode ahead to join Luke and Jolene at the front of the drive.

Laura turned to another cowboy riding nearby. He was wearing a blue-check shirt and had a wisp of dry grass sticking out of his mouth. "Who was that?" she asked.

The cowboy stopped chewing the grass for a moment. "Oh, that's just old Red. He hasn't been on a cattle drive for ages, but he sure knows how to ride."

He didn't seem surprised that Laura had appeared out of nowhere to join the drive. "What's your name?" she asked the cowboy boldly.

"I'm Hank," said the man. Just then, one of

the cows began to stray out of line, and he rode off to herd it back.

Laura watched him as he neck-reined his pony to and fro, guiding the cow back to the others without upsetting her. Hank made it look so easy! Laura felt a thrill of delight. She was on a real-life cattle drive with her own magic pony!

"We'd better stay in the background here," Star said quietly as they drew closer to the wooden buildings.

"Okay," whispered Laura. She leaned forward to stroke Star's neck. "Can anyone else hear you speak?" she asked.

Star shook her mane as though she was shaking off flies. "No," she replied. "To everyone else, it just sounds like neighs and whinnies. It's a special part of the carousel's magic—you picked the ticket with my name on it, and now we can understand each other!"

Laura grinned. What a fantastic secret! "So what's the important thing that we have to do?" she said, remembering what the pony had said earlier. "Was it saving the calf?"

"I don't think so," said Star. "If it was, the Magic Carousel would have taken us back to the fairground by now. I expect it's a bigger task than that. We'll find out what it is together."

A bigger task! thought Laura. *Wow!* Now Laura had something to use her detective skills on—she would keep a sharp eye out for whoever it was needed their help. But then she thought about her brothers, and suddenly felt worried. "But how long will it take?" she asked. "Won't my brothers notice I've gone?"

Star twitched one ear. "You don't need to worry," she said reassuringly. "When you go back, no time will have passed at all!"

Laura was thrilled. She wondered what her brothers would say if they could see her. It felt as if she was in a cowboy movie all her own!

Chapter 4

They reached the little cluster of wooden houses, and Laura tried to look as though she rode down the main street every day. But there was so much to look at! There were a few houses, a general store, and a saloon bar—but not a single car! Laura could hardly imagine riding on a pony to get everywhere all the time. Near the bar, a young woman in a long dress was pumping water from a long-handled tap into a bucket. Laura watched the woman dip a tin mug into the bucket, then offer it to Hank as he rode past.

Hank thanked her and gulped down the water as if he was very thirsty. Laura saw Luke and Red ride up to the hitching rail by the saloon and dismount. She watched them carefully. Instead of taking both feet out of the stirrups at once, they swung themselves out of the saddle with their left foot still in place. Laura copied them, trying to look as casual as possible—but as she stepped down, she stumbled backward and bumped into Jolene's pony.

"Careful!" snapped Jolene. "Smoky's jumpy enough today, thanks all the same!"

"I'm sorry," said Laura.

Jolene looped Smoky's reins over the rail. "It was your fault that the calf jumped into the river," she told Laura over her shoulder.

Laura looked at Star in surprise. The calf had been startled when Smoky kicked the stone! Star gave a tiny shake of her head that only

Laura could see. Laura knew she shouldn't quarrel with Jolene—the Magic Carousel hadn't brought her here to argue! She decided not to say anything about Smoky's mistake.

"You should have roped the calf as soon as he left the herd," Jolene added. She finished tying Smoky's reins and walked off toward the water pump.

Laura sighed. It looked like Jolene was determined not to make friends. She stroked Star's soft muzzle, then reached up and rubbed the little white star on her forehead.

"Don't worry about Jolene," said Star. "She's probably just jealous because you rescued the calf and not her."

"What do you think I should do now?" Laura asked, feeling slightly nervous.

"You'll be fine," said Star. "Just get a quick drink and come back here. You'll be thirsty

later if you don't."

Laura walked over to the water pump. The other cowboys had finished drinking. Laura drank a mug of refreshing water, then skipped back to Star.

All around her, the cowboys were climbing back onto their ponies.

"Let's go!" said Luke. "There's some wild country to get through before we reach the next camp."

Laura climbed into Star's saddle. "Shall we follow them?" she whispered. It was hard to know if they needed to go with the cowboys to find out their special task, or if they should stay behind in the little town.

Star scraped her front hoof on the ground as if she was thinking. "I think we should go with them," she said. "After all, I am a cowgirl's pony!"

Laura and Star cantered after the others. They

soon caught up with the long line of cattle stretching into the distance. Up ahead, the rolling grassy plain ended in a line of rocky hills. Laura felt a flicker of excitement. That must be the wild country that Luke had mentioned!

But as Laura joined the back of the drive, Luke cantered over to her, frowning. "Hey, Laura!" he called. "You'll have to go back to the village now."

Laura's heart sank into her cowboy boots.

"We have a long way to go with these cows," Luke went on. "And I only take the most experienced cowboys and cowgirls on my cattle drives."

Laura thought quickly. She had to persuade Luke somehow! "My mom and dad said I could join the next drive that passed through," she said. She gave Luke a pleading look. "*Please* let me come."

Just then, there was the sound of hooves as another cowboy rode up. "What's going on here?" asked Red in a friendly voice.

Luke explained, and Red smiled. "I think you should let her stay," he said. Laura's heart flipped over hopefully. "She saved the calf, remember?" Red reminded Luke. "She's obviously a good rider, and she could be company for Jolene, too."

There was a tiny moo from beside Star, and Laura looked down to see the little calf trotting along close to Star's flank.

Red chuckled. "You see, Luke, you can't send her back. That calf has adopted Laura as his new mother. She'll have to keep an eye on him from now on."

Luke watched the calf for a moment, then smiled. "You're right, Red. I can't send her back now."

"Thanks, Luke," said Laura. "I won't let you down, I promise."

She looked at the calf. He stared back with big, adoring eyes, then mooed again. Laura smiled. He might not know it, but this time the calf had saved *her*! Now she had a special calf as well as a magic pony. She couldn't believe her luck!

As Red rode on ahead with Luke, the old cowboy turned and gave her a big wink.

On they rode, across the plains, with the rocky hills slowly drawing closer. The cowboys spread out along the line of cattle, keeping them from straying too far off the trail. It was hard work, because the cattle kept wandering off to graze on any tasty bit of grass they saw!

The land began to change. Instead of swaying grass, Laura noticed prickly pear cactuses and boulders and bright yellow desert flowers. As they rode through a rocky canyon, she saw a lizard slither between some stones and a hawk fly overhead on the hunt for jackrabbits. And all the time, the calf trotted along close to Star. Laura smiled at her loyal new friend.

"I think we should give the calf a name," she said to Star. "What do you think we should call him?"

Star arched her neck and blew gently on the calf's ears. The calf twitched his ears happily. "Something to do with how you saved him?" she suggested.

"How *we* saved him," Laura corrected her, laughing. "How about River?"

"Perfect!" agreed Star.

As daylight faded the men set about making a camp. The cattle were allowed to stop and graze, and Laura made sure that River was settled among them. A young cow with a white patch on her nose sniffed at River, then let the little calf graze next to her. Feeling relieved, Laura rode off to join the rest of the cowboys As she dismounted, she couldn't believe how stiff she felt! She had never spent so long on a pony before, and traveling across country was very different from trotting around a field in a riding school. But she wouldn't have missed a moment of the amazing adventure she'd had so far.

Star nuzzled her, and Laura wrapped her arms around her pony's neck.

"Thank you, Star," she whispered. "This has been the best day of my life."

Star gave a happy whinny, then butted her with her nose. "You need to rest," she told Laura. "It'll be another long day tomorrow."

But Laura was too excited to sit down. She

watched as some of the others unbuckled bedrolls from the backs of their saddles and laid them out on the ground. But Star didn't have a bedroll behind his saddle—what would Laura do? The ground looked very hard and uncomfortable. Then she saw Luke pass Jolene a bedroll and nod in Laura's direction. Jolene didn't look very happy, but she started to walk over to Laura.

"Here. You can borrow this one," Jolene said in a quiet voice, handing the bedroll over to Laura. It was a beautiful striped red, yellow, and blue blanket.

"Thank you!" Laura said, hoping that Jolene might be feeling more friendly. Jolene gave a thin smile and walked away. Laura watched her leave, then laid her blanket out near the horses, so that she could sleep close to Star. Then, after making sure that Star had plenty of food and water, she set off to explore the camp. She had learned the

names of all the cowboys during the long ride, and already she felt as if she was part of the team.

Luke and Red were slowly riding around the cattle, keeping an eye on them, while Carlos the cook was unloading cooking equipment from the back of a pack mule. Tex and Mark were making a fire, with Jolene helping them. It was quickly getting cold now that the sun had set, and some of the cowboys wrapped themselves in colorful blankets when they sat down. Carlos began stirring a big pot of beef and bean stew on a smaller fire. It smelled delicious and Laura suddenly realized how hungry she was. She offered to help, and Carlos produced a stack of tin plates from one of his saddlebags.

"You can help me dish out," he said.

Laura gave Jolene a plate of stew first.

"Thanks," said Jolene without looking up.

"What about Luke and Red?" Laura asked

Carlos, when everyone had some food.

"Don't worry about them," Carlos told her. "I'll leave some stew in the pot and they'll eat when their shift's finished."

Laura felt a bit sorry for them—they must be really hungry! She sat down to eat her stew, thinking that being a cowboy was very hard work.

After a while, Laura noticed Jolene slip away to lie down in the shadows. Leaving the other cowboys sitting around the fire, Laura went over to her bedroll and snuggled down wrapped in her warm blanket.

"Good night, Star," she whispered.

"Sleep tight," her magic pony replied softly.

As Laura dozed off, she heard the sound of singing. At first, she thought it must be the men around the fire, but then she realized that it was coming from where the cattle were grazing. It was Luke and Red, singing to them as they rode around! Laura smiled and began to drift deeper into sleep.

Suddenly, a voice nearby jolted her awake.

". . . prices will be good enough," she heard.

Laura opened her eyes. The singing had stopped. She had no idea how long she'd been asleep. Perhaps Luke and Red had finished their shift by now.

"It will be easy money," said a muffled voice.

Laura felt her skin begin to prickle. There were definitely men talking nearby. And they weren't casually chatting—they were talking in urgent whispers, as though they were making a plan.

Laura lay as still as she could under her blanket, listening.

"Just need to wait for half the cattle to go into the ravine," said one of the men.

"The secret valley near that ravine is going to

be really useful!" said another. "We'd never be able to steal the cattle without it."

Laura's heart began to pound. Had she just overheard a plot to steal some of Luke's cattle?

Chapter 5

Laura heard the men walk back toward the fire. They passed close to where she was lying, and she held her breath. Suddenly one of them muttered crossly.

"What's wrong?" asked a companion.

"Nothing," replied the man. "Just a stupid cactus scratching my hand."

As the footsteps went past, crunching on the dry earth, Laura heard the rattling chink of a spur. She thought there were three men, but it could have been four. Her mind was racing.

The men's voices had been muffled by her blanket, which was tucked up around her ears, so she hadn't recognized any of the speakers. All she had were two tiny clues—one of the men had scratched his hand, and another was wearing a loose, jangling spur.

She heard the sound of one man mounting a horse, or maybe two. It was so annoying not to be sure! Laura wondered if Star was listening, too, but she didn't dare call out to her. Soon, the sound of singing started again, drifting on the night air. The rest of the camp grew quiet, and Laura peered out from underneath her blanket. She'd have to wait until morning to talk to Star. She stared up at the millions of stars stretching across the clear night sky. Only one thing was sure: all three or four speakers had been men.

At last, Laura drifted off to sleep again. When she woke up the gray-pink light of dawn streaked the sky. There was a chill in the air, and she shivered. Sitting up, she pushed aside her blanket and tiptoed over to Star.

The cow pony was dozing, resting one hind leg, but she woke up as Laura approached and whickered a friendly hello.

"Star!" whispered Laura, stroking her nose. "Last night I heard some of the men talking. I think they're planning to steal some of the cattle. Did you hear anything?"

Star pricked her ears. "No, not a thing. What happened?"

Quickly Laura told her everything. Star listened, her nostrils flaring.

"I think I know which ravine they're talking about," she said. "I overheard some of them talking about the route ahead yesterday. There's one place where the trail gets really narrow."

"That must be it," agreed Laura. "What can we do? I don't know who was talking about the plot—though they were all men, so that rules out Jolene."

Star tossed her head. "Well, maybe you should talk to her."

"But I don't think she likes me very much," Laura pointed out.

Star blew softly into Laura's blond hair. "She was the only girl before you came along," Star reminded her. "Maybe she just needs some time to get used to you."

"We don't *have* time," said Laura. The camp was already beginning to stir. She could see that Carlos was lighting his fire to cook breakfast. "We'll get to the ravine today, and that's when the cowboys are planning to steal the cattle!"

"Well," said Star, "we'll just have to hope that's enough time for you to make friends with Jolene."

When the cowboys had finished their breakfasts, they packed up the camp and saddled their horses. Laura tried to strap her bedroll into place behind Star's saddle. It was difficult, because the buckles were stiff.

"Do you need a hand there, Laura?" asked a kindly voice.

Laura looked around. Jesse was smiling down at her from his mustang. She yanked on the stiffest buckle, and the leather strap slipped into place.

"I'm fine, thanks." She smiled back at him.

"Well, you let me know if you need help

with anything," he said.

He sounded so nice and friendly, and Laura hesitated. Surely he couldn't be one of the thieves? She needed to tell *someone*, and Jesse was just the sort of person she'd willingly trust! But just as she opened her mouth to speak, another of the cowboys rode close by and gave Jesse a friendly slap on the shoulder. Laura snapped her mouth shut again. She knew the slap might not mean anything, but all the same, it reminded her that *any* of the men could be thieves—even Jesse!

Laura swung herself into Star's saddle. River trotted over and greeted Laura with a friendly moo. Laura really wanted to check all the cowboys' spurs and whether any of them had a scratch on his hand, but it was impossible. The men quickly spread out around the herd, and with all the dust it was difficult to see anything clearly.

"You're right," Laura said to Star, patting the pony's neck. "I can't stop the thieves on my own. I'll have to speak to Jolene."

Chapter 6

The cattle began to move slowly onward. Laura spotted River in the middle of the herd, and she felt glad that he seemed happy to be with the cattle again after his scary experience the day before. She could see Jolene's shiny black pigtails up ahead and realized that now was her chance!

Laura nudged Star with her heels. "Let's catch up with Smoky and Jolene," she said.

"Good idea," Star said, and broke into a canter. They soon caught up with the other girl.

But as they slowed down to a trot beside her, Jolene turned to them with her eyes blazing. "What d'you think you're doing?" she snapped. "You'll panic the cattle, cantering through them like that."

Laura was stung. She and Star hadn't cantered through the cattle—they'd cantered around them! *Why* didn't Jolene want to be her friend?

Out of the corner of her eye, Laura spotted a few cattle that were straying, and she pushed Star into another canter to guide them back to the rest of the herd. Once they were safely in line, she trotted back to ride alongside Jolene again.

"Well done," Jolene said grudgingly. "Which ranch did you learn on?"

Laura wasn't sure what to say. She'd learned to ride at her local riding school, but she'd learned about Western riding from movies! She couldn't say *that*. She thought quickly. "Oh, a place called Shady Creek," she said casually. Well, it was *almost* true. It was the ranch in her favorite Western storybook.

"Never heard of it," said Jolene. She shrugged. "I guess it must be pretty good."

Laura grinned. She was glad to hear the other girl say something nice at last! She patted Star's neck. "Well, I wouldn't be much good without Star," she said, and for the first time, Jolene gave her a friendly smile.

It was too good an opportunity to miss. Laura took a deep breath. "I think some of the cowboys are planning to steal half the cattle," she said. "I heard them talking about it last night. They're going to use a secret valley near a ravine."

Jolene stared at her as if she was crazy, and

then laughed. "There's no secret valley around here. You must have been dreaming."

Laura's heart sank. Maybe she'd gotten it wrong. After all, Jolene knew the trail much better than she did.

But then Star tossed her head and gave a whinny. "If Jolene knew about the valley, it wouldn't be secret," she pointed out.

It was true. Laura knew she had to keep trying. "I'm sure I heard right," she insisted.

Jolene rolled her eyes. "My dad knows all these guys really well. He would never use thieves on his cattle drive," she said. She raised one eyebrow. "Maybe you think my dad's a thief, too?"

"No!" Laura protested. "I just know what I heard, that's all. There were three or four men speaking, and one of them had a loose spur. Another scratched his hand on a cactus."

Jolene shook her head disbelievingly. A big cow wandered out of line up ahead, and she kicked Smoky with her heels.

"Now what?" exclaimed Laura, watching Jolene canter away to round up the cow.

"You did your best," said Star. "We'll just have to think of something else."

"Something else!" Laura echoed in despair. "Some*one* else is what we need. I can't help at all. The carousel must have made a mistake!"

"No, no, that doesn't happen," Star said, shaking her mane. "The Magic Carousel always chooses the right person to help!"

But right now Laura didn't feel so sure.

The sun rose in the sky, and the air grew hotter and hotter. The trail began to narrow, with craggy rocks towering up on either side in deep yellows and reds, contrasting with the lovely blue sky.

"The ravine must be getting close now," Laura said to Star, who nodded her head in agreement. Laura felt butterflies fluttering in her stomach. Then she noticed that one of the cowboys had dropped back and was dismounting.

Laura raised a hand to shield her eyes from the sun and saw that it was Hank. She turned to Tex, the cowboy nearest to her. "Is Hank okay?" she called.

"Oh sure," replied Tex. "He's just fixing his spur. It got loose yesterday."

Laura gulped. Hank must be the thief with the clinking spur! "Star, what can I *do*?" she muttered.

"Stay calm," said Star. "The ravine's just up ahead."

Laura looked desperately around for Luke,

but he was right at the front of the herd, at the entrance to a narrow gap between the rocks. She saw him cup his hands around his mouth.

"We're taking the first cattle in!" Luke called. "Follow on behind, not too fast!"

He turned his horse and rode alongside the first cows into the ravine. Laura stared after him. Should she gallop up to Luke and tell him what she'd heard? While she was trying to decide, Tex wheeled his horse around in front of her—and as he did, Laura noticed his hand. It had a deep scratch on it!

Tex cantered off in a cloud of dust, toward Hank, who was still at the back of the herd. A piece of paper fluttered out of Tex's saddlebag as he cantered away. But Laura was too busy wondering what to do next to look closely at it. Everything was happening so quickly!

"Tex must be one of the thieves, too!" she whispered to Star. "Come on, Star. Let's go and talk to Jolene again. She's the only person we can trust!"

Chapter 7

Jolene frowned as Laura cantered up to her. "What have you heard now?" she asked. "Is my dad about to run off with everyone's horses?"

"No, Jolene, please listen," Laura begged her breathlessly. "Hank and Tex have gone right to the back of the drive. Hank has a loose spur and Tex has a scratch on his hand. They must be the cowboys I heard talking last night!"

Jolene still looked doubtful. For one awful moment, Laura thought she was about to ride away. "You've got to believe me!" she insisted. "I couldn't have dreamed all that. You must help me before it's too late!" But Jolene didn't seem to be listening. She pointed at a thornbush just behind Laura.

"What's that?" Jolene asked. "There's something caught in the branches!"

Star trotted over to the thornbush. It was the piece of paper that Laura had seen fluttering out of Tex's saddlebag. Laura leaned down and peered at the thick black writing. *"Cattle sale!"* she exclaimed. She snatched the paper from the bush, then trotted Star back to Jolene. "Look at this," she said, handing it to her. "There's a big cattle sale taking place tomorrow. The thieves must be planning on selling the cattle there."

Jolene's eyes opened wide as she read about the sale. "It's in a town on the other side of the hills," she muttered. She looked up in amazement. "You must be right. But I've never heard of a secret valley."

Laura felt a rush of relief that Jolene believed her at last. "We have to stop the thieves!" she declared. "Let's go and warn your dad!"

Jolene looked down the line of cattle that were walking steadily forward, and Laura followed her gaze. There was no sign of Red, Carlos, and Juan—they had all followed Luke into the ravine.

"We can't," Jolene whispered.

Laura frowned. "What do you mean?"

Jolene looked very worried. "We can't warn my dad or Red or any of the others. They've already gone into the ravine."

Laura was puzzled. "Can't we catch them? We

could ride along the top of the ravine and canter down ahead of the cattle."

Jolene shook her head. "The sides are too steep and rocky. You can't canter down them, and even if we could, we might scare the cattle."

Laura gulped. She looked around. There were only four cowboys left at the back of the herd—Hank, Tex, Jesse, and Mark. As Laura watched, Hank and Tex left the others and cantered to the ravine entrance. They walked their horses into the mouth of the narrow gap, stopping the rest of the cattle from walking through.

Jolene's blue eyes flashed in anger. "They're dividing the herd in half!" she exclaimed.

As the cattle milled about in the entrance to the ravine, Jesse and

Mark began to guide them away from the main trail toward the hills.

Laura wheeled Star around. "Come on, Jolene! We'll stop them ourselves!"

Chapter 8

Side by side, Laura and Jolene galloped up to Hank.

"Hank, what d'you think you're doing?" Jolene shouted. "You can't steal the cattle. You'll never get away with it!"

Hank looked surprised just for an instant. Then he threw back his head and laughed. "Too late!" he hollered. "There's nothing you can do to stop us!"

Laura heard Tex laugh as well, and she felt a surge of anger. But she and Jolene couldn't turn the cattle around by themselves, not with four cowboys to stop them from trying!

As the last of the cows plodded after their stolen companions, Hank and Tex cantered off behind them, waving their hats in a mocking salute.

"So long, Jolene!" called Tex.

Jolene's cheeks flushed scarlet in fury. "We'll follow them!" she declared. "We must be able to stop them somehow!"

She urged Smoky forward, and he jumped straight into a gallop.

Star shook her mane. "I think we need to come up with a plan," she said.

Laura agreed. She stared at the rocky hills ahead of them. The cattle were disappearing one by one between a gap in the rocks. That must be the entrance to the secret valley!

"Wait!" she shouted after Jolene. "Come back!"

Looking annoyed, Jolene cantered back.

"Come *on*!" she said. "We can't let them get away!"

"I know," said Laura. "But we have to try to get in front of the herd. There won't be room to get past once they are in the secret valley." She pointed at the hill beside the narrow gap. "But if we could climb up there, we might be able to overtake them."

Jolene stared at the hillside. "That hill's pretty steep," she said doubtfully.

"I can manage it," whinnied Star.

Laura gratefully stroked the mare's neck. Star was so brave and loyal! "I think we should try," she said to Jolene. "Once we're ahead of the cattle, we'll be able to ride straight at them. They'll turn around in panic and we'll be able to drive them back down the valley."

Jolene thought for a moment. "It might work," she said at last. "Let's go!"

***

The two ponies began to pick their way up the side of the hill, puffing and blowing as they struggled up the rocky slope. When they reached the top, a cooling breeze blew against the girls' cheeks. Laura steered Star carefully along the ridge and looked down into the secret valley. It almost made Laura feel dizzy! There was the line of cattle, plodding along with the cowboys riding beside them. Laura took a deep breath. It was so beautiful here—exactly how she'd always imagined it from her favorite movies. But she wasn't here to enjoy the view. They had to stop the thieves!

The ponies trotted along the ridge until they had overtaken the cattle far below. Laura's stomach turned somersaults all the way. She desperately hoped the cowboys wouldn't look up! Fortunately, the cowboys were too busy guiding the cattle to spare a glance at the ridge above them.

Once the two girls were well ahead of the herd, Laura began to look for a good place for their ambush. They needed a gentle slope, so that Smoky and Star wouldn't stumble as they galloped down. At last, they found the perfect spot, just around a bend in the valley. All they had to do now was stand still . . . and wait.

The girls listened, waiting for the sound of cattle's hooves. The valley was silent apart from the shrill cry of a hawk. Laura gripped her reins more firmly. *We can do it,* she told herself.

Suddenly, Jolene pointed down the valley, where dust was beginning to rise in a pale yellow cloud. "They're coming!"

The first cow appeared along the track, with two more close behind . . . then two more . . . and there was Hank, riding alongside them.

Laura patted Star's neck. "Any minute now," she whispered.

Jolene stared down at the herd of cattle. "I still can't believe they're doing this to my dad," she muttered. "If he loses half the herd, no one will ever use him as a trail boss again. They're supposed to be his friends!"

"I know," agreed Laura, watching the line of cows get longer and longer. "But we're going to stop them, I promise."

Jolene nodded, her eyes sparking with determination. There was a pause, then—

"NOW!" both girls shouted at once.

With a snort, Star plunged down the slope toward the cattle. Smoky followed, and the girls waved and hollered at the tops of their voices.

"Wooo-wooo-wooo!" yelled Laura, waving her lasso above her head. "Go on, Star!"

Star galloped toward the first cows, her mane

blowing in the wind and her nostrils flaring. The cows stared at her in alarm—then started bellowing in fear. In seconds, the whole herd was leaping and scrambling around, fighting to gallop back the way they'd come. Laura caught sight of Hank and Tex. Their horses had panicked when the cows started stampeding, and both were rearing up, their front hooves pawing the air. Laura just had time to glimpse the cowboys struggling to stay on—and then all she could see was dust and cattle thundering past, out of the secret valley and back the way they'd come.

"We have to get to the front!" yelled Jolene. "We have to slow them down before they reach the ravine!"

There was only one way to get to the ravine ahead of the frightened cows, and that was to gallop straight through the middle of them.

The cows were stampeding already, so for once it didn't make any difference that Laura wasn't riding carefully around the edge of the herd. She clung on as Star surged forward, leaping over boulders and bushes. Laura didn't have to tell her what to do at all—the clever cow pony already knew! Out of the corner of her eye, Laura could see Jolene and Smoky galloping through the cattle as well. Jolene was slightly ahead of Laura.

After a few breathless minutes, Laura and Star arrived back at the main track and joined Jolene. She was calming the cattle down as they emerged from the secret valley by cantering in front of them and calling to them in a soothing voice. Laura copied her, and at last they managed to bring the cattle at the front of the herd back down to a trot.

"Try to let them into the ravine a few at a

time," called Jolene. "That way they won't hurt themselves."

Laura and Star blocked part of the way, so that the cattle trotted past her one at a time or just two by two. They eyed Star nervously, but she now stood still and calm with her ears pricked.

Laura let out a long sigh of relief. "We did it!" she called to Jolene.

"We sure did!" Jolene agreed.

They followed the last of the cows into the ravine. Laura looked back to see if the thieves had come out of the secret valley yet, but there was no sign of them. Suddenly Luke galloped around a corner up ahead. Laura guessed he had realized half the herd was missing.

"Dad! We rescued them!" called Jolene, waving at him over the backs of the cows. Luke listened in amazement as Jolene told her dad everything that had happened. "It was all Laura's idea!" she finished.

Laura smiled happily. "This was our task, wasn't it?" she whispered to Star.

The cow pony tossed her mane so that it flicked lightly against Laura's fingers. "Yes, and we did brilliantly!" she whinnied.

There was the sound of hooves behind them, and Laura twisted around in her saddle to see the four thieves cantering into the ravine. They pulled their horses to a halt when they spotted Luke. Laura held her breath, waiting to see what would happen next.

Luke started to gallop over to the thieves. "Hey, you!" he said. But before he reached them, the four cowboys turned their horses and raced away in a cloud of dust.

Luke slowed his pony and trotted back to the girls. "They won't get away with this," he promised grimly. "When we reach the next town, I'll make sure everyone knows what they tried to do. No one will use them on a cattle drive again, and they'll be in big trouble when the sheriff catches up with them!"

Laura exchanged a delighted grin with Jolene. With the help of their brilliant ponies, they'd saved the herd!

Later that night, around a roaring campfire, Laura sat next to Jolene, wrapped in her striped blanket. The camp felt small now that there were only four cowboys left, but Luke said he would be able to find more drivers when they reached the town.

Carlos cooked an extraspecial meal to celebrate, and Juan played lively tunes on his violin for the girls to clap along to. River the calf left the herd for a while and came to stand behind

Laura and Jolene as they sat together on a log. Laura felt a bit worried. She and Star had saved the cows, but what would happen to River when the Magic Carousel took her home?

Just then, River ducked his head down and nuzzled his nose into the back of Jolene's neck. Jolene laughed and reached up to stroke his furry brown ears. And suddenly Laura knew River would be just fine without her, because Jolene would always look after him.

Next morning, Laura woke up when Red shook her gently by the shoulder. It was another beautiful day. Sleepily, Laura packed away her bedroll and took it over to Star.

"Hello, Star," she whispered, stroking her warm chestnut neck. She knew that today would be her last day on the cattle drive, now that they had finished their task.

As they rode, the trail began to widen, and the cowboys passed other riders and a few rickety chuck wagons, throwing up clouds of dust from their wooden wheels. Laura patted Star's neck and peered through the dust at Red, who was riding a little way ahead. The sunlight glinted on a metal buckle on his hat, and Laura felt as if she was in a golden haze of sparkling light.

Snatches of music began to play, and Laura looked around, puzzled. Where was it coming from? Then she realized that the hot dusty plain had faded away and she was surrounded by twinkling lights, flashing in pretty pink colors. The Magic Carousel came smoothly to a halt and Laura looked down. Star's neck was no longer soft and warm. Her body and mane were made of painted wood once more. But her chestnut ears were still pricked, and as she slid out of the saddle, Laura was sure she heard her give one last little whinny.

Laura reached up and touched the pony's little white star. "Thanks so much," she whispered.

Her bangs fell across her face and as she pushed her hair back behind her ear, Laura felt something. She pulled it out and looked down at it in surprise. It was a stem of prairie grass! Laura closed her fingers around it, picturing the endless grassy plains. Riding on the cattle drive had been the greatest adventure of her life, and now she had something to remember Star by forever!

Chapter 1

"Got it!" Sophie waved her long bamboo pole. It had a yellow plastic duck swinging madly on the hook at the end.

"Well done!" said her mom.

Sophie's dad unhooked the duck and handed it to the woman standing on the other side of the inflatable pool. Lots of bright yellow ducks bobbed on the water, waiting to be hooked. The woman smiled at Sophie and told her to choose a prize.

Sophie picked a key-ring in the shape of a pretty jet-black pony with a tiny white dot on its forehead. She loved ponies more than anything else in the world! "Thank you!" she said to the woman running the stall.

Beside her, there was a crash as Sophie's little sister Molly threw down her bamboo pole. "This is a stupid game!" Molly grumbled. "I can't hook any of the ducks. They keep swimming away!"

Sophie sighed. Molly was only four, and she got very cross when she couldn't do everything Sophie did.

"Let's go and find something else," said their dad. He took Sophie and Molly by the hand and they wandered further into the fair. It was very busy, and Sophie held tightly to her dad's hand. She put her other hand in her pocket to check her pony key-ring hadn't fallen out. The little jet-black pony felt warm and smooth underneath her fingers.

There were rides and stalls *everywhere*! Sophie thought she'd never be able to decide what to go on next. Her mom pointed to a stall where you had to kick a soccer ball into a goal to win prizes. But Sophie didn't think she could win a better prize than her pony key-ring, so she shook her head.

Just then, she spotted a pointy golden roof peeping out from behind the soccer ball game. Tugging her dad's hand, she led him over.

"Look!" Sophie cried. "It's a pony carousel!" It was the prettiest fairground ride she had ever seen. The wooden ponies were really lifelike, their eyes twinkling and their tails floating out behind them.

"Would you like to have a turn?" asked Sophie's mom.

"Yes, please!" Sophie said. There was nothing

she wanted more than to ride around on the carousel, holding one of the twisty golden poles.

But Molly had spotted something else. "I want to go on the giant teacups!" she said, pointing.

Sophie stared at her sister in surprise. How could giant spinning teacups be better than the beautiful pony carousel? Molly started to drag their dad towards the teacups. Sophie felt a bit cross. Now she wouldn't be able to go on the carousel!

Her mom bent down and gave her shoulders a squeeze. "Shall we stay here while your dad takes Molly on the teacups?" she said. Sophie nodded eagerly.

She walked to the bottom of the steps leading up to the carousel. There were so many ponies! There was a stocky white pony with a stiff mane and bells and ribbons on his harness—the kind of pony Sophie had seen pulling sleighs in pictures.

Then she spotted a handsome bay pony with brave brown eyes and a tail that flowed all the way down to the floor. He had an old-fashioned saddle as though he was a medieval knight's pony.

Then Sophie gasped out loud. One of the ponies looked exactly like her key-ring! He was jet-black—the color of a dark, velvety night—and he had a perfect diamond of white on his forehead. When Sophie peered closer, she saw a little name-scroll hanging from the golden pole on his back. It read, *Jewel*! It was the perfect name for such a beautiful pony.

Someone coughed politely close by, making Sophie jump. A tall gentleman was standing behind her. He was grandly dressed in a red velvet suit and a red-and-green striped top hat. He bowed to Sophie, sweeping the hat from his head.

"Welcome to Barker's Magic Pony Carousel!"

he declared. His blue eyes twinkled. "My name is Mr. Barker."

Sophie stared at him. "Did you just say *Magic Pony Carousel?*" she said.

Mr. Barker grinned. "Oh yes! Most definitely magic. Would you like a ride on the carousel?"

"I'd love to!" Sophie gasped.

"Well, I have just a few tickets left for the next ride," he said. He reached into his pocket and took out some tiny pieces of pink paper. "The name of your pony is written on the ticket you choose, Sophie. Think hard about which pony you'd like it to be!" Mr. Barker held out the tickets to Sophie, along with a magnifying glass. "Pick one! And have a look at it with the magnifying glass. The writing can be a little hard to read sometimes," he explained.

Sophie thought hard about the midnight-black pony that looked like her key-ring. Then with trembling fingers she chose one of the little pink tickets. She lifted the magnifying glass and peered at the tiny piece of paper. The swirly writing was hard to read—but it definitely said Jewel.

"It's Jewel!" she told him excitedly.

"Ah! That's a very special pony." Mr. Barker beamed. "Now, quickly, on you get, we're ready to start. Climb aboard, everyone! All aboard the Magic Pony Carousel!"

Sophie ran up the steps and weaved her way through the other wooden ponies until she reached Jewel. "I'm so glad your name was on my ticket!" she whispered, stroking the white diamond on his forehead. The painted wood felt silky under her fingers. Jewel's dark eyes seemed to look straight into hers, as though he was glad, too. Sophie gave him a quick kiss on the nose, then climbed into the saddle.

Mr. Barker checked that everyone was on

their pony before he twirled a big golden handle to start the carousel. There was a grating noise, then music rang out, and Sophie felt Jewel soar into the air as the carousel moved off. She gripped the golden pole tightly and waved to her mom as she whirled past her. The fairground slipped by in a blur of silvery-lilac light, the tinkling music filled Sophie's ears, and the crowds seemed to fade away.

Sophie blinked. The other girls on their wooden ponies had vanished, too, and she and Jewel were galloping through swirls of sparkling mist. The sunlight dimmed until they were surrounded by velvety black shadows. . . .

Suddenly, Sophie knew they weren't in the fairground anymore!